mini S·A·G·A·S·

Fiction From Scotland

First published in Great Britain in 2008 by
Young Writers, Remus House, Coltsfoot Drive,
Peterborough, PE2 9JX
Tel (01733) 890066 Fax (01733) 313524
All Rights Reserved

© Copyright Contributors 2008
SB ISBN 978-1-84431-581-9

Foreword

Young Writers was established in 1991, with the aim of encouraging the children and young adults of today to think and write creatively. Our latest secondary school competition, 'Mini S.A.G.A.S.', posed an exciting challenge for these young authors: to write, in no more than fifty words, a story encompassing a beginning, a middle and an end. We call this the mini saga.

Mini S.A.G.A.S. Fiction From Scotland is our latest offering from the wealth of young talent that has mastered this incredibly challenging form. With such an abundance of imagination, humour and ability evident in such a wide variety of stories, these young writers cannot fail to enthral and excite with every tale.

Contents

The Mini Sagas

Noises

A loud *bang!*
Eventually, curiosity took its grip.
Slowly, ears pricked, I slid up the stairs.
Alone in the house, it was my duty to investigate.
Glass bottle in hand, I rounded the corner,
ready to attack. I saw the culprit; a book from
the shelf, motionless, on the floor.

Graham Thomson (15)
Eastwood High School, Glasgow

11

The End

Something was happening, it was nearby, it was everywhere. In the alleys, in the streets, the world was changing. No soul thought it would end this way. Happiness was taken over by shock. A momentous day like this was bringing the world to a halt. Happy New Year. World's End.

John Scott (14)
Eastwood High School, Glasgow

The Audition

Breathing heavily, I tiptoed cautiously
into the room, smothered by swarms of confident
ballerinas. Feeling like the smallest person in the
world, I crept towards the crowded bar.
Suddenly, music exploded in my ears, excitement
burst into my heart and butterflies fluttered inside
my stomach. Adrenaline powered my movements.
Ecstasy!

Laura Pasternak (15)
Eastwood High School, Glasgow

Life's A Game

I stand all alone in the mysterious forest.
No birds, no animals. I look around and see nothing
but looming trees. The leaves crunch under my
weight, as I walk cautiously through dark nature.
Gunshots and explosions I hear in the distance.
Life pauses. I set down my controller.

Scott Sutherland (15)

Eastwood High School, Glasgow

14

The Figure

A shadow at the bottom of the bed,
a figure standing tall, staring. She closed her eyes,
wishing she were imagining it. She waited. Slowly,
she opened her eye. He was still there. He was
clutching something, something big. Switching on the
light quickly, she looked up. It was Santa.

Amanda Keenan (15)
Eastwood High School, Glasgow

15

My First Fish

The float plunged under, suddenly, the pond was full of life. The water surrounding shot up and splashed back down into the pond. There was a silence, something glimmered beneath the surface, then disappeared. Seconds later, a shiny salmon leaped violently onto the shore. I had caught my first fish.

Stephen Daffy (15)
Eastwood High School, Glasgow

Midnight Sky

The eerie silence fascinated onlookers,
darkness sweeping across the stars. Then *flash*,
bang and *sizzle*. Colours bouncing through the air,
dancing for the pleasure of others. The sky alight
with magic and wonder, reflecting in young children's
eyes. Then an explosion, everything fell.
Remember, remember the fifth of November.

Abby Paterson (15)
Eastwood High School, Glasgow

The Falling Dream

The icy air conditioning was surrounding
me, suddenly I was falling. The plane's floor
abruptly vanished to leave me spiralling towards
the ground, getting closer every second.
The air ran through my hair. I jolted as I hit the ground.
The floor of the plane returned. I was safe again.

Stephanie Downie (15)
Eastwood High School, Glasgow

Birthday Surprise

The car turned the corner, I could hear
my heart beating in my ears and couldn't believe
my eyes. The engine of the hot pink Hummer roared
and the ground shook with the thudding music.
I stumbled over to my best friend, 'Take it
we're not getting the train then?'

Rachel McNaught (15)
Eastwood High School, Glasgow

The Waves

I watched the waves, each one growing
bigger, stronger and wilder than the last … until I
felt the water pull me in. The coldness of the sea
shocked me. I gasped for breath as my soaking wet
clothes pulled me down. Panic filled me as
I sank lower … and lower …

Jacqueline Stables (15)
Eastwood High School, Glasgow

Trapped

I was wondering, waiting, thinking. I sat, hoping,
praying, hurting. I looked around, trying to find a
way out. I was trapped, trapped by hateful lies.
Nobody's fault but my own. I wasn't ready to die.
It was one small mistake that spiralled out of control.
Or was it?

Sadia Naeem (15)
Eastwood High School, Glasgow

Ballet Butterflies

As I pulled the satin ribbons on my ballet shoes together tightly, a strange sensation took over my body. It was a weird feeling, a feeling I had never felt before. I could hear the excited crowd chatting away, noisily, in the audience. My heart started racing. I was ready.

Hollie Whyte (15)

Eastwood High School, Glasgow

22

Christmas Time

Snow, everywhere I looked. Excitement filled
the frosty air. Lights, sparkle, glitter decorated the
magnificent trees. The children, tucked up in bed,
but not one of them asleep. They were anxiously
waiting for Christmas morning to arrive.
In the distance they could hear Santa,
'Ho, ho, ho, merry Christmas everyone.'

Gaile Weston (15)
Eastwood High School, Glasgow

23

Uncaring Counsellor

'I don't like my new stepmum.'
'Change is difficult for children.'
'She's horrible to me.'
'We all wish parents would stay together.'
'She doesn't let me do anything.'
'It must be hard for her too.'
'She kills kittens and puts them in my bed.'
'You'll understand when you're older.'

Clare McCafferty (15)
Eastwood High School, Glasgow

The Dark

Darkness swept across my room, features lost
in the shadow, my world went black. I was trembling.
My senses were alerted, I could hear every miniscule
noise, like a floorboard creaking or the rush of the
wind outside. I never thought I would escape.
Someone turned the light back on.

Claire Johnstone (14)
Eastwood High School, Glasgow

Back To Square One

Climbing Everest was treacherous,
but the snowy peak was rapidly approaching.
Eventually I realised it wasn't me moving impossibly
quickly but an avalanche.
While climbing a tree I stupidly hoped it would simply
skim past underneath. But the tree toppled and I
hurtled to the bottom, where I started again.

Shona Noble (14)
Eastwood High School, Glasgow

The Snowman

The harshness of the heat, the blinding rays.
The sun cruelly beating down, attacking the man,
like daggers penetrating his melting exterior.
He was composed of three mighty lumps of snow
clumped together. Dying, as the great ball of fire
slowly devoured him, leaving pools of icy remains.

Anupria Kaur (15)
Eastwood High School, Glasgow

Stephen Paffy

It wasn't cold that woke little Emily from
her dream, it was noise. Excited, she
stumbled silently through static darkness.
Her heartbeat rose as she approached the sitting
room and continued to rise as little Emily's eyes met
the eyes of a figure, not dressed in red but black!

Kenneth Cormack (15)
Eastwood High School, Glasgow

Le Maison

Intrigued by its peculiar appearance, he entered the sandstone building. A solid oak door, an incessant staircase. More doors, single pane windows the only source of light to the forgotten dwelling. As he walked his pace quickened, faster, faster. Suddenly, the once solid floor beneath his feet crumbled, he fell.

Jonathan Dawson-Bowman (15)
Eastwood High School, Glasgow

Disease Boy

There once was a boy, so unclean,
who was also particularly mean. His skin looked
slimy and green, his appearance was more the
obscene. *But don't worry!* He lived his life as a dream.
In his world, he was king, but he still smelt
of rancid tuna mixed with herring.

James Weston (15)
Eastwood High School, Glasgow

The Forgotten

It was dark. The door creaked
menacingly as it gently pushed open.
The room was large, empty, yet full of silence.
The fireplace reminisced of long dead embers.
Dust, unsettled by my footsteps, fell like snow.
I shouted. Echoes bounced back like
the house's own words.
This is my house.

Nichola Philp (15)
Eastwood High School, Glasgow

Snowmen

There are two snowmen in a field.
One of them huffs and says, 'Why is it so boring?'
The other says, 'I know.'
They both stand, melting in the sun.
Eventually, one of them says, 'Is it just me,
or can I smell carrots?'
The other says, 'Ha! Ha!'

Caffum Tonner (14)
Eastwood High School, Glasgow

The Sea

The waves came in rapidly as a figure emerged from the sea. Limping his way through the waves he headed for the sand, while all the people on the beach fled. Once he reached the sand a massive wave appeared and swept him back into the sea.

Laura Wood (15)
Eastwood High School, Glasgow

Blink, Shoot, Failure

'No, hold on!' The gunshot escaped into the distance. A blink and it was gone. It hopped into the tangled roots. Hunch-backed, I trudged back to the looming silhouette of my house. 'No dinner today,' I mumbled to the towering figure of my ever-demanding wife.

Hiba Hameed (15)
Eastwood High School, Glasgow

FA Cup Final 1972

Leeds United went to Wembley in the spring of '72.
Billy Bremner being captain we sank the Gooners
and won the Cup. Bremner held high the Cup with
rosy white ribbons glistening in the sun.
Those days are gone now, but Leeds United
will rise again.
Glory, glory Leeds United.

James Hill (15)
Eastwood High School, Glasgow

Pancake

Up, up and away, the chocolate cake flew
and did a 360 degree spin in the air. *Splat!*
It fell to the ground. *Vroom!* The car ran it over.
A new way of making a pancake is invented!

Olivia Wong (15)
Eastwood High School, Glasgow

Cold Summer

The cold was biting at my ears. The sharp wind piercing my cheeks. The night depressing, gloomy and still. My shadow unseen, for I was alone. In the background dogs barked like madmen. The cold angered them, their breath fogging the air. This was during the winter in Scotland.

Michael Bass (15)
Eastwood High School, Glasgow

37

The Classroom

Sitting here now, thinking about
all the creative, exciting ideas. Listening to the
grumbles and moans of confused pupils.
Five minutes go by.
Nothing!
I try to sneak a peek at the boy next
to me, can't see anything.
Well, I should get started on
a maximum of 50 words.

Andrew Jackson (15)
Eastwood High School, Glasgow

The Room

I walk in slowly to my pitch-black house. The door left wide open, inviting anyone in. I walk slowly down the corridor to face my door, I open it slowly. There's a thud, I rush in, I look in the corner, see a figure standing still, watching me.

Dayse Ritchie (15)
Eastwood High School, Glasgow

No Sweat

'Do that one more time and I'll bite your fingers off!'
an English voice warned.
Another boy walked up to him and hit him!
The first boy jumped at the withdrawing hand.
Red flashes.
Impurity.
The boy screamed, Reynold smiled viciously and
spat out four bleeding plump fingers.

Carol (14)
Eastwood High School, Glasgow

Aeroplane

The plane flew at ten miles per hour.
Slowly taking off before steadily hitting an
altitude of seven feet. The witnesses were excited at
the success of this magnificent vehicle. The
noise; there wasn't any. The colour; white.
It began to rain, it dissolved!
Paper aeroplanes aren't that much fun!

John Forbes (15)
Eastwood High School, Glasgow

At The Seaside

I feel my feet sinking into the warm sand, as I am walking down the beach. There is a sharp scream as a girl is trying to go into the cold sea water. I am glad that I am only sunbathing today.

Angus Erskine (15)
Eastwood High School, Glasgow

Demons

It was the carnival in Venice and
everyone had on masks of demons.
Two people dressed as demons, a man and
a woman, met and decided to go home together.
The man took off his mask.
'Now you,' he said.
'I'm not wearing a mask', she said, and killed him.

Rebecca McKenzie (15)
Eastwood High School, Glasgow

Christmas Eve

It's the night before Christmas and here in the flat,
drunk Uncle Angus goes doon with a splat. Dad's on
his doak, watching big mannies play darts. Dozy auld
Granda just lies doon and farts.
Mam, as usual, sits there and glowers, because
wee bairnie Bobby's been spewin' for hours.

Alan Henderson (14)
Fraserburgh Academy, Fraserburgh

44

Murder!

The blade glistened in the dull light as I lifted the knife above my head. I was shaking. The knife plunged down. *Chop!* Blood squirted out onto my shirt. I couldn't believe what I'd done! Cutting meat is no job for a vegetarian.

Luke Tait (14)
Fraserburgh Academy, Fraserburgh

Best Day Of The Year

It was so exciting. The anxiety was unbearable.
I had been waiting all year. One day to go.
Everyone was waiting.
Finally, the day came. I walked over …
and opened my Advent calendar.

Rachel Gordon (14)
Fraserburgh Academy, Fraserburgh

Burning Eyes

I see it, the flames burning in the trees.
The roaring blaze comes closer. My heart beating
with excitement. My eyes widen as it appears before
me. The warm air brushing across my face,
soft and cuddly.
My little ginger cat has found me.

Andrea Rex Carter (14)
Fraserburgh Academy, Fraserburgh

Great Escape

Running! Running! I couldn't escape. They were catching up. How could I keep going? But there - my escape was in view. I was safe. I'd escaped past the finish line. Oh, how I hate sports day.

Rebecca Gray (14)
Fraserburgh Academy, Fraserburgh

Disastrous Disco

Standing on the dance floor, the nice guy was over there. I'd spent all week deciding what I should wear. I prayed that the sequins didn't make me look like a Christmas tree! I tried a smile - hoped it would work, but then I realised … I'd tucked in my skirt!

Jemma McLean (14)
Fraserburgh Academy, Fraserburgh

Tree Ring

I spun the tree round for the umpteenth time. Soon it would fall, coming off its stand. I spun it again, it fell out of my ear. It was only an earring after all.

Heather McRobbie (14)
Fraserburgh Academy, Fraserburgh

Cluck!

For months he watched and waited. I knew it would be soon, as December approached. Which day would be my last? I trembled at the thought of spring never arriving. God, I wish I wasn't a turkey!

Rachel Whyte (14)
Fraserburgh Academy, Fraserburgh

Splat!

It was defenceless. Dropped from high above
onto sharp, revolving blades. The bright red juices
flew everywhere. Flesh covered all of the walls.
I forgot to put the lid on the blender again.
My strawberry smoothie - ruined!

Jozie-Anne Smart (14)
Fraserburgh Academy, Fraserburgh

Bright!

I ventured outside and was blinded by all the colours. There were reds, purples, greens and golds. All different shapes and sizes, all along the street. Those stupid Christmas lights!

Effen Bruce (13)
Fraserburgh Academy, Fraserburgh

Gunshot

My heart was beating wildly. I stopped breathing to steady my aim. I pulled the trigger, there was a bang and the endangered species lion fell to the ground. I had shot a tranquilliser dart to calm the lion down.

Ewan Massie (14)
Fraserburgh Academy, Fraserburgh

Destruction

There it was, perched proudly in all its glory. It was so beautiful, shiny and glimmering in the mesmeric lights. Then, *rip, tear, slash*, my brother got hold of the big, shiny Christmas present.

Jack Walker (14)
Fraserburgh Academy, Fraserburgh

Alone

He sat in the dark cupboard, forgotten by all.
Everyone else had been evacuated. There was a
low rumble approaching. He waited, in the hope he
would be saved. But the school would be demolished
long before the last textbook was remembered.

Rosa Berry (14)
Fraserburgh Academy, Fraserburgh

A Memorable/ Unmemorable Night

It was brilliant. Everyone was having fun.
I was going to remember this night forever.
Now I am broke, no job and no family. My clothes
are rags and my best friend is imaginary.
I have learned my lesson.
Don't drink and drive.

Kristoffer Ritchie (14)
Fraserburgh Academy, Fraserburgh

Prowfer

Walking through the grass. It's long and wet.
It's sticking to me as I wander through the trees.
I see a shadow moving through the trees. A growl
and moan, a movement through the grass. I stand
frozen, when suddenly, it jumps out, pounces on me.
It's Scampi, my cat!

Naomi Drummond (12)
Fraserburgh Academy, Fraserburgh

Sleep Walking

I am running across the court as fast as I can,
then I jump and score a basket. Everybody's
cheering for me, shouting, yes, yes, yes!
Then I awake, I notice I am hanging from a tree
with someone confused looking up at me.

Jordan Reid (12)
Fraserburgh Academy, Fraserburgh

A Dark Night

It was getting late. She had to go home.
The phone rang and there were just the two of us.
Bang!
She was gone - no traces left. I woke up screaming!
It was only a dream, or was it?

Kimberley Barclay (12)

Fraserburgh Academy, Fraserburgh

The Deep Pool

I'm swimming for my life. I'm getting closer to the side. I am drowning, I am sinking but I try to swim back up. I make it. Just as I'm about to reach the side … my mum came in, 'Come out of the bath, you've taken ages!'

Daniel Mowat (12)
Fraserburgh Academy, Fraserburgh

Murder

As I pressed against the wall even more,
I saw the man's knife glint in the moonlight. I tried
to scream but no sound came out my mouth. As the
man advanced, the air tasted foul in my mouth
and my life flashed before my eyes.
I woke up screaming.

Jessica McCfure (ll)
Fraserburgh Academy, Fraserburgh

That Boy

That day, that boy, that moment. She looked into his eyes. She knew it was him. The right boy to ask. As she sat under the tree, a boy approached her. About to pop the question, she interrupted him, saying, 'No, I was staring at him!' as she pointed strongly.

Lindsey Harper (13)
Fraserburgh Academy, Fraserburgh

Exercise Dilemma

Someone started chasing me. I jumped
on a bike and started pedalling. It did not move.
No matter how hard I tried, it wouldn't move. They
were getting closer. I pedalled, nothing happened.
Their voices boomed, 'Don't work too
hard, you'll hurt yourself.'
Turned out it was an exercise bike.

Catherine Metcalfe (12)
Fraserburgh Academy, Fraserburgh

Wrong Thing!

At school, I got up off my chair for a pencil.
The teacher came over to me with a ring.
I said, 'Oh, I didn't expect this to come, but
… yes, of course I will marry you.'
'Is this your ring by any chance?'
I felt so stupid.

Amy Stuart (12)
Fraserburgh Academy, Fraserburgh

Wrong Person!

I was in the line for lunch, when this boy
came over and said, 'Will you go out with me?'
I immediately said yes!
He then said, 'I wasn't talking to you, I was talking to
Amy.' She was the girl standing in front of me.

Devin Macinnes (12)
Fraserburgh Academy, Fraserburgh

The Goal

Champions League Final: I played for Rangers - it was against Barcelona. It was 0-0. It went to extra time. It was still 0-0 at the 120th minute. I scored a great goal - top corner. Everybody cheered. It was a great feeling, until the linesman said it was offside.

Eddie Thomson (13)
Fraserburgh Academy, Fraserburgh

The Car Of My Dreams

I've been saving for years.
Now I have enough. It's mine, the car of my dreams.
I go into the showroom, I hand the money over, he
shows me it. It is shiny and new. It is ready to go.
I will take it out of its box later.

Joseph McCallum (13)
Fraserburgh Academy, Fraserburgh

My Gorgeous Poster

This is the best time of my life, Jesse.
Oh Jesse, I love you. I can't believe I'm kissing you.
Oh no, not again, I've got to stop kissing this poster.

Shaun Reid (12)
Fraserburgh Academy, Fraserburgh

The Visitor

Lying in my bed, it's pitch-black.
I hear loud noises coming from the roof.
Please, oh please, I think to myself. The noise
gets louder, I hear a man's deep voice.
'Thank God, Santa's come this year.'

Amy Jane Birnie (16)
Fraserburgh Academy, Fraserburgh

Angels

Bored in the classroom, I looked out
of the window. To my surprise a choir of angels
descended into the courtyard of the school.
Flapping their wings, cawing - rucdy seagulls!

Geordan Wood (16)
Fraserburgh Academy, Fraserburgh

71

The Figure

Who was this mysterious figure?
Tall and broad but cold and shivering violently.
Then I heard him, an old friend, murmuring my
name. I could see him, at the end of this daunting
alley ahead. He looked different somehow,
something had changed since I saw him last.
'George?'

Bryony Shepherd (14)
Fraserburgh Academy, Fraserburgh

First Crush

As I walked happily along the street,
I saw my crush, the boy of my dreams, walk
towards me. He gave me a playful smile and waved
casually. I waved my arms excitedly but soon
realised he'd waved to the girl behind me.
Whoops, I felt like an idiot.

Rachel Summers (16)
Fraserburgh Academy, Fraserburgh

Jimmy's House

There was once a guy called Jimmy.
He stayed in the biggest mansion in town.
No one liked him because of his greed for money,
so one day some villains went to his house secretly
and smashed all his windows. One stone hit Jimmy.
He wasn't to get hurt!

Greg White (12)
Gleniffer High School, Paisley

Rat Attack

'Argh!' Something just bit me.
I struggled to get my torch. 'Got it. Rats.'
The rat reacted to the light and bit harder this time,
piercing my skin. I saw more climbing onto me,
slowly eating my flesh away. I shook myself free and
stumbled away with mangled facial features.

Sam Egan (12)
Gleniffer High School, Paisley

Sleigh

One day a man called Santa went
to check on his sleigh. It was not there but then, up
behind him, he felt a nudge. It was his sleigh. Rudolph
had run away to play in the snow with it. Santa felt
relieved, he gave Rudolph a big hug.
Aww!

Kirstin Harrigan (13)
Gleniffer High School, Paisley

Broken Soul

Once a boy called Bob fell down the stairs and broke his leg. The ambulance came. He had to go into surgery for five hours. When he got out he was still asleep, so we don't know how he is. We will have to wait and see how he is.

Dale Smiley (13)
Gleniffer High School, Paisley

77

The Monster In The Wardrobe

George opened his wardrobe to get his coat.
Stood before him was a big purple monster, with
spots on his nose. George ran downstairs shouting,
'Mum, there's a monster in my wardrobe.'
Mum went upstairs with George and
looked in the wardrobe.
'I can't see anything,' she said.

Robert Cockburn (12)
Gleniffer High School, Paisley

The Yeti

'The yeti is alive I tell you, alive.'
'How is it? It's a myth.'
'No, I will take you to its footprints
up in the mountain.'
'He is telling the truth. Follow them.'
He takes them to a cave.
'Look, a big white thing.'
'Argh! It's the yeti, run!'

Kyle Wilson (12)
Gleniffer High School, Paisley

The Miracle

Once upon a time, in an unusual land,
there was a girl called Robyn. Her stepmother was
very evil to her. Robyn's dad died when she was eight.
One day she decided to run away. She eventually
came to a big mansion. Her dad wasn't
dead, he was in there.

Laura Thomson (12)
Gleniffer High School, Paisley

The Bomb

One day the school blew up.
The police got to the scene. They found out there
was a bomb in the janitor's room. The only suspects
were the janitor, head teacher and the cleaner.
The bomb went off at 21.50 and the
head teacher was killed.

Daryl McNeiff (13)
Gleniffer High School, Paisley

The Shadow

She ran faster and faster, it still followed.
When she stopped, it stopped. When she ran, it ran.
Every day it was always there. Rain, hail or shine.
It followed her everywhere. She knew it would
always be there with her.
She later found out it was her shadow.

Blair Ruane (13)
Gleniffer High School, Paisley

The Black-Caped Man

As I ran through the dark forest, the black-caped man was still following with terrific speed. I felt my life running out, as if it was a clock. As I saw the school gates, the man, viciously, pulled me back and said, whilst panting, 'Here's your lunch money, son!'

Ryan Lee (13)
Gleniffer High School, Paisley

The Famous Bush

It was Hallowe'en. As I walked home from school, I heard a noise from a bush, but I just walked on. I could hear it at every bush. It was getting louder. It was following me! I began to run but it got faster too. Darkness overtook me. Help!

Christopher McKiffop (13)
Gleniffer High School, Paisley

War

Bullets flying. Guns firing. It's simply war. People dying. Blood flying. Babies crying. It just won't stop. Airstrikes coming. Terror, burning. Bombs incoming. It's now time to run. The final target. Everyone's watching. Impact incoming. The silence of horror creeps around the corner. Everyone's dead. Now who is to blame?

William Twaddle (13)
Gleniffer High School, Paisley

Nightmare

George was running, it was behind him.
It was dark. He was in a forest. It had already
killed everyone, there was nowhere to go.
George could hear it coming, closer and closer.
It had caught him, it plunged its claws into him.
Then everything went black, he woke up.

Scott Ferguson (13)
Gleniffer High School, Paisley

It's Been So Long

How long have I been here? In this cell?
It feels like years since I saw sunlight. I can't
remember why I'm here any way. I have to
remember, so I can right that wrong. I wonder how
my family is doing and if they are still alive.

Alastair Wylie (13)
Gleniffer High School, Paisley

87

The Night

It was night, dark, alone and scary. I lay in my bed with my eyes wide open. Noises started as a shadow brushed against the window. I was really scared. The noises started getting louder. I stood up and walked towards the window, to realise it was only a tree.

Amanda Gilmour (13)
Gleniffer High School, Paisley

The Execution

A huddled figure, broken-spirited, stands surrounded yet alone. Back bent, head down, limp, almost lifeless. Breathing, shuffling crowds bustle and scrap en-masse. Multitudes of filth, without decency or honour. Gasps and exclamations. Silence, then a hollow thud. Nothing but the stench of death and the steady drip of blood.

Rose Hadshar (14)
Kelso High School, Kelso

A Colourful Life

Two seconds before, she had been so happy,
surrounded by her friends of many colours.
Suddenly, she was the chosen one. Her heart
was broken, her legs snapped. Then nothing but
darkness. Down, down, down, until there was no
return. A life cut short. The agony of a jelly baby!

Caroline Lunday (12)
Largs Academy, Largs

Gardening

Lights flickered as the sun set. The sky was pink and red. The sky turned to black, with stars like diamonds hanging in the night sky. The leaves rustled in the breeze. The flowers went droopy without any sun. The wind whistled through the trees.
I hate doing the gardening.

Georgia Woods (12)
Largs Academy, Largs

The Crocodile Chase

It was the sunniest day of the year,
Fred the croc was lying on his rock like a
speed bump on a road, not moving an inch.
Suddenly, he started running. Behind him was
a man, following as fast as he could.
Fred turned, *Grrr!*
Fred pounced.

Richard Ward (13)
Largs Academy, Largs

Rose Fairies

I looked at the circle of roses. Fairies were flying about like dust falling through the sky. I could be a fairy. If I was a fairy I wouldn't have any problems. They said, 'Come, play.'
As soon as I stepped into the circle of roses they turned to thorns.

Dania Grant (13)
Largs Academy, Largs

Rudolph The Red-Nosed Reindeer

Rudolph was anxious. Santa was about to choose the reindeer for delivering presents. Rudolph hadn't been picked yet and was nervous. This year, Santa realised the sky was foggy. He saw the light and selected Rudolph.
He exclaimed, 'Thanks Santa!' and set off merrily, when suddenly his nose dimmed.

Ryan Brown (12)
Lasswade High School, Bonnyrigg

The Final Hole

It is down to the final hole,
he has to get a birdie to win The Open.
Poulter's drive goes straight down the middle
of the fairway. The 7 iron approach lands 10
feet away from the pin.
This is to win The Open.
He sinks it! He's the champion!

Marc Fairman (12)
Lasswade High School, Bonnyrigg

The Door

Two kids were walking through the house, when they found *the door!* They were curious and decided to open *the door!* Their bodies were never found but their names were written in blood on *the door!*

Douglas Thomson (12)
Lasswade High School, Bonnyrigg

96

Rudolph, the Multicoloured Nose Reindeer

Rudolph awoke and saw that his nose was green,
'Darn that annoying green elf,' he said to himself.
Mrs Claus tried to get it off but nothing would work.
Then she remembered, she bought *Daz*, she tried it.
Like it says on the tin, the stain was removed.

Taylor Halliday (12)
Lasswade High School, Bonnyrigg

My End

I stand on top of the cliff, watching it. The island.
It was unknown what lived there. I'm stuck here.
Footsteps are coming towards me. Why don't I want
to run? The footsteps are getting closer now.
It's too late.
Then he pushes me. I'm falling, falling to my end.

Olivia Bird (12)
Lasswade High School, Bonnyrigg

Lost

Icy wind blew through my hair. I couldn't
see because the snow was blowing everywhere.
'Hello, hello …' I cried.
No answer. I was alone, none of the
people I came with were around. I was out
in the open, at the South Pole.
No civilisation, I was scared and lost.

Chloe Renwick (12)
Lasswade High School, Bonnyrigg

The Sleigh Of Christmas Eve

Bells jingled, as a large, colourful sleigh sped along the snow. Suddenly, it's lifted off the ground by a group of reindeer. At the front, a red light flickered. As it disappeared into the distant sky a jolly, 'Ho, ho, ho!' echoed on the lifeless tundra below.
It was gone.

Lewis Oliver (12)
Lasswade High School, Bonnyrigg

The Dragon

The dragon blew. Crimson red came blazing towards me, barely missing me. He flapped his wings and blew out. Fire came cascading towards me. I jumped; everything went black. I woke in his lair and my eyes met his. He picked me up, opened his mouth … Then I woke up.

Scott Cummings (12)
Lasswade High School, Bonnyrigg

Pineapple Disaster

Zunga and Joobjoob were aggressively trying to get some pineapples off the tree. They tried climbing it, shaking it and throwing rocks at it. Nothing worked. In the end they gave up and went back to their five star hotel to have some coffee.

Calum Davidson (12)
Lasswade High School, Bonnyrigg

The Red Sea

I felt its teeth sink into my flesh
and it crunched my bone. I saw the water turn
a dark red. I could only make out its teeth.
The pain was so unbearable. I held my breath.
I gave up. There was no way I could beat the shark.

Caitlin Wood (12)
Lasswade High School, Bonnyrigg

Dreams Can't Come True

Before I knew it, I was running alongside some of the
best players in the world. The light of the day blinded
me, as I stepped out onto the vast, green pitch.
Fans screaming my name …
'Blair, Blair, get up! You're late again, you're so lazy!'

Blair Paul (13)
Lasswade High School, Bonnyrigg

Out The Window

'Sophie, I have to tell you something,'
said Sophie's Mum.
Sophie could tell this wasn't going to be good news.
'You know Santa comes every year, well …'
said Sophie's mum.
There's another belief out the window!

Mairi Macdonald (12)
Lasswade High School, Bonnyrigg

A Christmas Shock

I woke up and looked out the window,
it was snowing. I rushed down the stairs and
to my surprise I found no presents. I wondered
what was going on, so I looked out the window
to find Santa lying, holding his leg.
What had happened to Santa?

Erin Scanlon (12)
Lasswade High School, Bonnyrigg

Luc The Elf

The North Pole is where Luc lives.
'Luc, good work this year,' said Santa.
'Thank you,' she replied.
All day long she had a great big smile on her face.
As she walked towards the hall of toys everyone
clapped and it made her day very happy.

Ashley Noble (13)
Lasswade High School, Bonnyrigg

Ally The Angel

The light was blinding. The light was shining.
It was a beautiful angel.
'I'm Ally,' the angel softly said. 'What is your wish?'
My wish is for me and my family to have
a great and jolly Christmas.

Tamara Davidson (12)
Lasswade High School, Bonnyrigg

Where's My Carrot

I lay in my bed on Christmas Eve.
I heard a knock at my window.
'Who is it?'
I opened my curtains.
'Ah, it's, it's …'
'Rudolph,' said Rudolph.
'What's wrong?' I asked.
'You left Santa biscuits and milk, where's my carrot?'
'Sorry,' I said, 'I'll try to remember next year.'

Shereen Maxwell (13)
Lasswade High School, Bonnyrigg

War Story

The sirens went off above my head. I got up and ran through Edinburgh faster than a cheetah. I heard the bombs starting to fall. I kept on running and a bomb hit me. I was dead before I hit the ground. The bell rang and I closed my jotter.

Aidan Robertson (13)
Lasswade High School, Bonnyrigg

Santa Dust

Smash! Bang! Crash! What was that?
I suddenly woke up. I ran through to my sister.
'Santa's here.'
She jumped out of bed. We ran downstairs to
see sparkling dust dropping from the chimney.
'Santa dust,' I said.
'Quick, quick, grab it, it's magic dust,'
said my little sister.

Rachel Hall (13)
Lasswade High School, Bonnyrigg

The Suit

Lying in bed, I heard a thud. The Christmas feeling was all around. I sat up to see what the thud was. An old man, there in front of me. I switched the light on. Instead of a red suit, it was black. To my surprise it was a burglar!

Chelsey Barton (13)
Lasswade High School, Bonnyrigg

The Sword Story

I roam through the night, sword held tight, always looking behind me. I fight my battles only if there's someone close to me. My horse leads the way, there's no one to stop me. I travel with one companion, the only one who knows me, the bravest knight of all.

Connor Dunlop (13)
Lasswade High School, Bonnyrigg

113

What Was That Noise?

There was a bang. I woke up. It was coming from down the stairs. I went down, there was someone stealing my Christmas tree. I jumped on him. It was a giant block of living cheese. I sliced him up and had a cheese toastie!

Matthew Smith (13)
Lasswade High School, Bonnyrigg

Day Of Infamy

The cold got to us all, I was terrified.
Everyone shivering and throwing up over the sides.
'30 seconds,' said the driver.
Eventually the ramp fell and all of a sudden, *bang,
bang!* Off went the 50. I heard a hiss as
I fell and I knew no more.

Stuart Easton (13)
Lasswade High School, Bonnyrigg

Peter's Kitchen Nightmares

Peter Potato sat looking at the fridge door, Lenny
Leek had already been taken, he was next. What
awaited him beyond the fridge? Where would those
hands take him? The fridge door opened, the hands
came for him, closer and closer they came till …
Argh! Wow! What a scary dream.

Lynsey Dolan (13)
Lasswade High School, Bonnyrigg

Santa's Night

Christmas Eve, in my bed, all I could hear was the
whistling of the wind. Suddenly, I heard sleigh bells,
so I looked out my window and saw a skinny man
and thought, Santa's lost lots of weight.
He saw me and threw a mint at my window.
It smashed!

Lisa Fraser (13)
Lasswade High School, Bonnyrigg

Porthole To Lapland

Kaboom! I was in my room but now I am in a
workshop, a small one indeed. Surrounded with a
happy atmosphere, with little people with pointed
ears and funny costumes. They told me,
'Sit down and get working. We've one hour till …'
I suddenly awake, sweating, in a hospital.

Robyn Martin (12)
Lasswade High School, Bonnyrigg

118

Pink Jump

Down the slope I went. Skiing to my heart's content.
I saw a jump ahead, I took to the air. A cold draught
hit my legs, I looked, people pointed and laughed. I
looked down, my pants were pink and fluffy.
'They're my wife's,' I said.

Connor Norris (13)
Lasswade High School, Bonnyrigg

Christmas Tree

I'm prickly and stiff. People see as an object at Christmas. They try to make me special. They put baubles, stars, tinsel and lights on, they don't realise I'm hurt, they don't realise that I belong in the open, where I can feel the cold frost on my needles.

Chloe Wilson (13)
Lasswade High School, Bonnyrigg

Lost And Found

She rushed about furiously, in a hurry, opening every drawer, every box, every cupboard, but still no phone. Screaming with anger, she began to sob and slouched onto her bed. Completely stressed, she squeezed her fists together and then she felt it …
She giggled, the phone was in her hand.

Stephanie Tamburro (13)
Lasswade High School, Bonnyrigg

121

Santa, The True Story

It was unusually quiet for December; all elves asleep.
Suddenly, Santa started singing. *Drunk again,* thought
the elves but what they didn't know was the sack of
toys wasn't bought or made, but stolen!
Santa's now on the run again. Police are saying he's
stolen over £10,000,000 worth of toys.

Nicky Cameron (12)
Lasswade High School, Bonnyrigg

I Thought I Saw Santa Claus

'Suzan, wake up! I hear sleigh bells.'
Suzan and Karenna walked towards the door,
made their way to the kitchen. They looked
through the glass door and walked in.
'Karenna, Santa's in there!'
They went in but it was just Karenna's dad,
sipping at the milk and eating the cookies.

Gemma Gulland (13)
Lasswade High School, Bonnyrigg

The Star Of Bethlehem

I was flying through the woods one day, when
I saw a light shining so brightly in the sky.
'It's the star of Bethlehem,' I said.
As I got closer it got brighter. It had a blue glow.
'Don't fly towards the light!'
Ssszzzz, too late.
'Bye, Benjie the fly!'

Danielle Rankin (12)
Lasswade High School, Bonnyrigg

Midnight Dreams

The wind howling against the window woke me up. I sprang up in bed, I heard a creak. I went into the hall and down the stairs, it was cold. I got to the bottom and there it was, the answer to all my dreams …

Joanna Jenkins (13)
Musselburgh Grammar School, Musselburgh

Undercover Kid

As a kid, working for the FBI, I was alone.
I walked down a dark, candlelit alleyway,
I saw a dark figure near some steps.
He pulled out a 9mm pistol. *Bang!*
A sniper bullet caught him in the temple,
whilst I was already entering a coma!

Joshua Struthers (12)
Musselburgh Grammar School, Musselburgh

The Game

The sun was shining on Easter Road and I was sitting
watching the game from the dugout. We were losing
one - nil against Celtic and it was a very tight game.
At half-time the manager gave me the nod to get ready.
'Wake up Neil, breakfast is ready!'

Neil Watson (12)
Musselburgh Grammar School, Musselburgh

Game Cancelled

It felt like the clouds were touching our heads,
they were so low and dark. Great drops of rain
landed heavily and dripped off the ends of our noses.
We trudged back over the squelchy, waterlogged
pitch, our boots clogging up with mud.
Game cancelled due to the weather.

Euan Greig (12)
Musselburgh Grammar School, Musselburgh

Hidden Identity

A body was discovered in caves, in the mountains of Italy.
The journalist was murdered. His body lay undisturbed
for years. Who was he? Who murdered him?
Inspector Gibbons travelled to Italy to investigate,
only to find that he had no identity. He didn't exist!
Will the case be solved?

Amy Johnston (12)
Musselburgh Grammar School, Musselburgh

Mortified Musings

I was at the toilet, around elevenish,
when I heard the fire alarm go off. All of us in
the bathroom rushed outside. I couldn't understand
why everyone was pointing and laughing at me.
Until I looked down and realised that my trousers
were still dangling around my ankles.

Rachael Stewart (12)
Musselburgh Grammar School, Musselburgh

Going Crackers At Christmas

'Thank goodness,' she sighed, 'these bags are so heavy.'
Christmas shopping had gone well. As she clicked the
car open she could relax. She sank into the driver's
seat, it was only then she heard the dog growl.
'Oh no! I'm in the wrong car!'

Caroline Slight (12)
Musselburgh Grammar School, Musselburgh

Climbing

A man called James Nisbet was going
climbing. When he got there he was scared, because
it was high but he went for it and started climbing.
He had everything he needed to climb.
Half-way up, at 500feet he lost his balance
and fell, never to be seen again.

Keith MacNeil (12)
Musselburgh Grammar School, Musselburgh

The Plunge

One afternoon, Laura was standing behind a diving block, waiting to swim the most important race of her life. She was worried. She started biting her nails. The starter blew the warning whistle. I thought she was about to faint. She stayed calm, the whistle went and she was off!

Emily Atkinson (11)
Musselburgh Grammar School, Musselburgh

That Icy Morning

As the low winter sun rose, Daniel was walking to school wearing a thick ski jacket. He strolled along the edge of the country road, listening to his iPod. Daniel's phone rang. Just as he answered his phone he heard a skidding noise. He turned around and … *bang!*

Jamie Cameron (12)
Musselburgh Grammar School, Musselburgh

The Crisp Cold Walk

Cold air swam down her throat as she
walked home. Rain battered down, when from
somewhere came a noise. She glanced round, her
hair dancing in the wind. A man, tall and dark, stalked
her. Starting to run, her heart began to pound.
'Wait!' she turned, 'You dropped your keys.'

Marei Binnie (12)
Musselburgh Grammar School, Musselburgh

The Shadow In The Dark

As I tiptoed through the hallowed hallway, the sound of dripping water made me shiver. I walked slowly towards the door. Where is the vampire? I sped up, quickly looking for the shadow of a person.
A loud *creak!* came from behind.
I span round, it was a mouse!

Robyn Grant (12)
Musselburgh Grammar School, Musselburgh

Keep On Going

I was running, faster and faster. I kept on going and couldn't stop. The footsteps were getting closer and closer as I got slower and slower. I mustn't stop now. I could hear voices now, getting louder and louder. I stopped for two seconds, when …
'Tig, you're it!' Oh no!

Lisa Burnside (12)
Musselburgh Grammar School, Musselburgh

The Open Door

An open door led me into an empty house.
It was odd that there was nobody in on my birthday.
I made my way slowly into the living room, it was
surprisingly dark … until an almighty,
'Whoop,' let fire, and, 'Surprise!'

Shannice Miller (12)
Musselburgh Grammar School, Musselburgh

Seasons

Last autumn, it was a beautiful sunny day, when I saw the tall, beautiful long-haired woman. She was picking the leaves off all the tall trees. She walked over to me and said, 'Hi, my name is Autumn.' Then she walked away and disappeared behind a large, beautiful tree.

Callum Gowans (13)
Whitburn Academy, Whitburn

Murder

She walked towards the altar, reaching
down and picking up a goblet of sparkling rubies
and emeralds. Drinking the violet liquid, she wiped
her mouth and strolled towards the exit.
Suddenly, she grasped her throat and screamed.
Finding it hard to breathe, she collapsed
on the floor, her heart stopped.

Affan Brodie (14)
Whitburn Academy, Whitburn

Untitled

Gripping my stomach, I slipped from consciousness.
As I woke I felt strange. I opened my eyes and as I
looked all around I had a sudden awareness of bright,
white light surrounding me. I then came back to reality
and then realised where I was. I was in Heaven.

Taylor Gilchrist (14)
Whitburn Academy, Whitburn

141

The Ball

Everyone froze to silence and turned to the back of the room. Their mouths dropped open and eyes widened as she walked through the door. Her dress flowed smoothly across the floor. The day had finally come that everyone had been waiting for - when the prince met his princess.

Chelsea Sneddon
Whitburn Academy, Whitburn

The Transformation

My nails started to bend backwards and rip off.
I grabbed my chest as I screamed out in pain. My
jaw dislocated and transformed into a snarling snout.
Razor sharp teeth and taste buds that longed for
flesh and the taste of sweet blood.
I was now a monstrous, terrifying werewolf.

Amy Smith (14)
Whitburn Academy, Whitburn

143

The Raging Sea

Crashing against the rocks with almighty
rage, throwing the ship back and forth violently,
making me feel sick. I feel like a ragdoll, being thrown
around by this massive bully, as soon as we left port.
This ride's been so uncomfortable and now
I know we'll meet our end.

Nicole McGrorty (14)
Whitburn Academy, Whitburn

144

Untitled

The crowds fell silent. Brother and sister hand in hand.
Tears streaming down mothers' faces and a look of
fear on many others. Then came a blinding light and a
worrying sound. People sat on the edge of their seats.
Then the word they'd all been waiting for came,
'Leon!'

Christina Currie (14)
Whitburn Academy, Whitburn

Meeting A Legend

Here I am. Here he is. The blue glow
of Stamford Bridge highlights our faces. I feel
tiny next to this 6 foot hero. He's my idol. Shaking
hands, he gives me his signed No 8 shirt.
He nods, ruffles my hair, then disappears
into the darkness of the tunnel.

Aimee McMahon (14)
Whitburn Academy, Whitburn

Untitled

It was late on Friday night. I was walking down a deserted pathway. Who would have expected cars to be speeding down a road at that time of night? As I stepped out onto the road I was blinded by a bright light. Then *bang!* and everything went quiet.

Amy Ferguson
Whitburn Academy, Whitburn

The Cloaked Figure

As I crept closer to the crack and peered through it,
someone screamed. By the time I got there, there
was just a steady trickle of violent, red blood.
Then suddenly, a cloaked figure swooped down
upon me and took my breath away.

Jordan McDonald (14)
Whitburn Academy, Whitburn

The End Of The Soul

I could see the light, shining through the door.
There was screaming, I could not see anything. It was
cold and dark out in the hallway. Screaming again.
I turned round then … blackout.

William Kerr (14)
Whitburn Academy, Whitburn

My Frog Jimmy

I had a frog called Jimmy, he hopped and hopped
around the garden all day. Until one day, to my surprise,
I looked in the garden to find that he was gone.
I cried and cried until one morning he was
sitting with a sly smile on his face.

Shona Garland (13)
Whitburn Academy, Whitburn

Lovely Chocolate

It was there. I had found what I had been searching for.
It was there, in front of me. The most precious thing of
all. The most important thing in my life. My lifeline, my
saviour. I had been looking for it for so long.
I found it, lovely chocolate!

Robyn Bonnar (12)
Whitburn Academy, Whitburn

151

The Loch Ness Monster

As I looked out over the glistening loch, I'd never felt so relaxed. Away from normality, of busy, rushing roads. There was a fisherman on the other side. Then everything happened at once. A big creature rose out of the water and splashed back in! Taking the fisherman too!

Lauren Pringle (12)
Whitburn Academy, Whitburn

The Amazing City

I was so pleased being here, blinding lights were everywhere. Buildings covered with advertisements for the LG chocolate. Even though I was only here for one day, I was still pleased to be here, in the middle of America, in the Big Apple also known as the colourful New York.

Rachel Kyle (12)
Whitburn Academy, Whitburn

Confused

I woke up, I was in London. I don't know how I got there but it was all snowy. The soft, delicate snowflakes were floating down gently onto my face. everything was a blur, all I could see was the city lights but I noticed everyone had disappeared …

Leonna Brown (12)
Whitburn Academy, Whitburn